FURIOUS DUSK

THE ANDRÉS MONTOYA POETRY PRIZE

2004, *Pity the Drowned Horses*, Sheryl Luna
Final Judge: Robert Vasquez

2006, *The Outer Bands*, Gabriel Gomez
Final Judge: Valerie Martínez

2008, *My Kill Adore Him*, Paul Martínez Pompa
Final Judge: Martín Espada

2010, *Tropicalia*, Emma Trelles
Final Judge: Silvia Curbelo

2012, *A Tongue in the Mouth of the Dying*, Laurie Ann Guerrero
Final Judge: Francisco X. Alarcón

2014, *Furious Dusk*, David Campos
Final Judge: Rhina P. Espaillat

The Andrés Montoya Poetry Prize, named after the late California native and author of the award-winning book, *The Iceworker Sings*, supports the publication of a first book by a Latino or Latina poet. Awarded every other year, the prize is administered by Letras Latinas—the literary program of the Institute for Latino Studies at the University of Notre Dame.

FURIOUS DUSK

For Allen —

May you always
find the words
you're looking for!

DAVID CAMPOS

University of Notre Dame Press

Notre Dame, Indiana

Published by the University of Notre Dame Press
Notre Dame, Indiana 46556
undpress.nd.edu

Manufactured in the United States of America

Library of Congress Cataloging-in-Publication Data

Campos, David, 1984–
[Poems. Selections]
Furious dusk / David Campos.
pages cm. — (The Andrés Montoya Poetry Prize)
ISBN 978-0-268-02377-5 (pbk. : alk. paper)
ISBN 0-268-02377-8 (pbk. : alk. paper)
1. Fathers and sons—Poetry. 2. Children of immigrants—Poetry.   I. Title.
PS3603.A49A6   2015
811'.6—dc23
2014044973

∞ The paper in this book meets the guidelines for permanence and durability
of the Committee on Production Guidelines for Book Longevity of
the Council on Library Resources.

For my parents

And for my wife

CONTENTS

Acknowledgments   *ix*
Introduction to the Poems by Rhina P. Espaillat   *xi*

I

Hunting   *3*
Fourth-Grade Lunch   *4*
Lion's Den   *5*
Cast Iron   *6*
To Sing   *7*
Soccer Practice   *8*
Drywall Dust   *9*
The Call   *10*

II

After One Year of Trying   *15*
Washing Dishes   *16*
Inheritance   *17*
Prayer   *19*
Hollywood Endings   *20*
Museum of Natural History   *21*
Skin   *22*
Need   *23*

III

Designated Driver   *27*
I Make My First Delivery   *28*
At the Entrance of a Back Alley   *30*
Monster   *31*

Molting *32*

A Wage-Claim Conference in Fresno *33*

At the Unemployment Office *35*

Wash *36*

Fences *38*

IV

Thirst *41*

Lizard Blood *42*

Stones *43*

Diet *44*

330-Pound Man Exercises *46*

Bowl *47*

Pica *48*

The Measuring Tape of a Dressmaker *49*

Last Words *50*

The Stones from the Water *52*

V

After Hearing of My Father's Passing *57*

Ars Poetica *59*

Where the Sirens Go *60*

Open Letter *61*

The Language of Masa *63*

I Left You a Note *64*

Addressing a Letter to My Father *65*

Birthday Dinner *67*

He Holds Out His Hands *68*

Lost Letter to Kees *69*

Dusk *70*

ACKNOWLEDGMENTS

I would like to thank the editors of the following magazines and journals where the following poems, and earlier versions of them, including under different titles, have appeared:

"Drywall Dust" and "He Holds Out His Hands" have appeared in *The American Poetry Review*.

"After Hearing of My Father's Passing" has appeared in *Boxcar Poetry Review*.

"Cast Iron" and "Where the Sirens Go" have appeared in *Connotation Press*.

"After One Year of Trying" and "Dusk" have appeared in *Huizache*.

"I Make My First Delivery" has appeared in *In the Grove*.

"Lost Letter to Kees," "Pica," "Fences," Lizard Blood," and "Addressing a Letter to My Father" have appeared in *Miramar*.

"Need" and "Thirst" have appeared in *Mosaic*.

"Hunting" and "Fourth-Grade Lunch" have appeared in *Oranges & Sardines*.

"Bowl" has appeared in *The Packinghouse Review*.

"Birthday Dinner" has appeared in *Plain Spoke*.

"A Wage-Claim Conference in Fresno" has appeared in *Solo Novo*.

I would like to thank the following people for their contributions, guidance, kindness, and support: My deepest gratitude goes out to my teachers. I will be forever thankful to Chris Abani for throwing me into the abyss and giving me the tools to climb back out, to Juan Felipe Herrera for leading me out of the forest and showing me what's possible beyond the pier, to

Christopher Buckley for not putting up with my bullshit and for all his help, to Tim Skeen for his support, to Robin Russin for his patience and kindness, to Goldberry Long for opening up language, to Lee Herrick for introducing me to poetry and to the work of Andrés Montoya, to Alex Espinoza for his guidance and for opening my eyes, and to Mikendra McCoy for believing in me.

This book wouldn't be possible without the support of my poetry brothers and sisters: Andrea Gutierrez, Jesus Leyva, Kathleen Kilcup, Angela Peñaredondo, Eric Loya, Scott Hernandez, Melisa Garcia, Michelle Lin, Kazumi Chin, Andrew Waddell, Kristopher Ide, Vickie Vértiz, Michael Torres, Fatima Mirza, Jared Robbins, Andre Yang, Brandon Williams, and the rest of my workshop colleagues.

A special shout-out goes to Greg Emilio, Rachelle Cruz, Ángel García, and Sara Borjas. We went through some serious shit together, and without you I'd be lost.

For being there at the beginning, for your kindness to the newest poet on the block, I'd like to thank Tim Z. Hernandez and his songs; Marisol Baca for the space, the food, and the poetry; Bryan Medina for doing what you do. And I'd like to extend this gratitude to Michael Medrano for your friendship, poetry, and all the shenanigans we got into.

None of this would have been possible without the support that I've received from my family. Pops, I love you. Mom, I love you more. Brothers, I love you most days. You've allowed me to dream, and I will never forget it.

Lastly, I would like to thank my wife, Courtney Campos, for her endless support and for her strength.

Writing is impossible to do without community. To all of those unmentioned, I'm thankful for everything.

INTRODUCTION TO THE POEMS

Selecting the 2014 Andrés Montoya Poetry Prize has been, for me, a privilege and a happy process of discovery: discovery, in general, of how rich and robust Latino poetry is in the United States at present; and, specifically, the discovery of a major talent in the author of *Furious Dusk*, the winner out of a remarkable field.

Let me say, before focusing on the winning text, that it was a pleasure to read these manuscripts by strong, talented authors representing our bilingual, bicultural experience and the immigrant legacy, whether lived, "inherited," or powerfully imagined. I enjoyed the variety of their work, the individuality of the multiple voices speaking the poems, the characters that people these pages, and the invitation that every one of these manuscripts extends into compelling stories I could not help but inhabit and learn from.

But the prize goes to the outstanding *Furious Dusk* by David Campos, a work whose five parts trace a son's effort—only partially successful—to fulfill his father's expectations and—perhaps even more difficult—understand those expectations enough to forgive them.

From the opening of Part I, a brutal hunting scene that plunges the reader into the book's pervasive violence, through the painful medical procedure during which the boy is commanded not to cry, to the growing man's endless efforts to do difficult, dangerous work without revealing the physical cost involved, the reader witnesses a life spent trying to become what his own nature does not accept, in order to please a severe father. There are references to beatings with a heavy belt that was "used to brand my body when I was loud and didn't follow his orders."

Part II introduces new disappointments perceived as personal failures: a marriage that falls apart, a long-awaited child not conceived month after month, illness, poverty, all conveyed through imagery that hurts almost physically. "My wife shifts in her sleep," we're told, "and I hear her teeth grind like a carcass dragged slowly over gravel."

Part III returns to the theme of family and losses, through memory and dreams in which the speaker's self-contempt is linked to history and binds an entire community. Race, a conflicted identity, demographics, violent encounters that leave hatred in their wake, and the desire for revenge all play a part in the mounting frustration of the speaker, who half-yearns for destruction. Watching a paralyzed woman smoke with her oxygen tank behind her, he hopes "the explosion will get rid of these skins I live in." And a series of poems dealing with attempts to appeal to social service agencies illustrates the futility of such efforts, and hints at "the murderous intentions of the dark."

Part IV travels in time in both directions, following the father's tortured life back to a Mexican childhood and an earlier generation, and forward into the speaker's own burden of obesity, his brother's alcoholism, and the failure of faith and human love to comfort him with what he calls "all illusions." But unexpectedly, at this low point, the son begins to speak *for* his father, as if finally able to internalize his father's past and read the thoughts of a figure who has worked on him like the two poles of a magnet.

Part V begins with "After Hearing of My Father's Passing," a poem that returns to the hunting scene with which the book opens, but with such hard-won wisdom that it redeems what precedes it by turning the work, not into a circle of haunting, inescapable repetitions, but into a spiral widening and opening up and out into a possible future. The act of writing, of confronting life through language that clarifies what it cannot change or justify, becomes the speaker's route to a new life of his own.

Now César Vallejo, Pablo Neruda, Philip Levine, and Weldon Kees turn up in epigraphs and references, as guiding spirits from both of the speaker's cultures. In a poem titled "Ars Poetica," the grown son finally recognizes his right to be who he is. New, wiser responses to life in his endangered community follow, and, in retrospect, loving "rearrangements" of memory that alter his appraisals of his father, his ancestry, his childhood, and himself. Are these truer perceptions of the past, or glosses to make acceptance of the past possible, or fantasies meant to comfort? Or all of the above?

I don't know, and I'm not sure it matters. Whatever the source of the transformation that takes place in the final poems, they illustrate the poet's capacity to make something out of any reality whatsoever, thereby touching upon the nature of poetry itself, and celebrating its role in our lives.

For me, *Furious Dusk* best fulfills what I consider the essential functions of poetry that works: it sets out to communicate; it sings what it means to say; it uses imagery, not to confuse and exclude the reader, but to draw him in.

And finally, it is not narrowly "Latino poetry," but rather effective poetry composed by someone who happens to be, among other things, a Latino, speaking of what he knows to readers both inside and outside his community, in ways that render his work universal and humanly relevant to others. My wholehearted congratulations to David Campos, whose name I am glad to learn: I hope to encounter it again soon, and often!

—Rhina P. Espaillat, *Judge*

HUNTING

We don our camouflage and walk quietly with rifles
up a mountain trail deep into a thick forest.
I carry the .30-30 my father used to kill his first deer,
the same deer mounted in our living room.

The huddle of shivering men whisper plans with twigs.
We spread out in a line, push through the forest
creating flanks. My chance to join the club of men
before me: a small four-point buck followed
by a doe and a young deer. I try to control
the small bounce in my breathing as I aim.
"Shoot it," my father whispers.

I hesitate, knowing what killing means,
having seen it before when an uncle shot a deer,
when it didn't buckle and die. We had to track it down.
The buck settled underneath a pine and struggled to breathe.
I remember its eyes, dark, so dark and brown.
My uncle, with his pistol, shot it in the head,

then dragged the body to a nearby tree where we hung it
and gutted it. Blood everywhere. The smell of shit.
I stopped believing in God.

I aim and fire. The family of deer disappears
as the bullet ricochets off a granite boulder.
The shot echoes off the mountains.

FOURTH-GRADE LUNCH

Phil, a scrawny kid, slings words
like dirt at my face—clods with rocks
inside scratching away at my skin.
I hear my father tell me not to walk away,
to stand there and chop away. Stand there
and bleed. And feel life like he did as a kid,
wet with anger, the word *bastard*

stinging his eardrums, a constant buzzing noise
his classmates wouldn't give up.
How he would swing his fists instead of words.
He shows me his tooth, the one that's chipped,
says this is not walking away.
I tell Phil, meet me in the restroom
during lunch recess. The restroom is small,

amazing how many kids come to watch.
I make them all laugh, pretend to be The Karate Kid
as Phil steps in and comes at me. His fists hit my face
and I cower, turn my back. I feel kicks on my legs and spine.
I cover my head and fall against the tile floor.
I weep. I hear one of the kids say "run"
and another call me a "pussy."

LION'S DEN

I'm surviving
    the lion's den
of high school.
    The blue dots
of balls popping
    off walls, off hands
of those I call friends—
    a bunch of posers
like me wearing red shirts
    & red belts & red shoelaces.

I'm called upon to hunt
    but I refuse
to follow the Blood
    beyond the handball courts
to the Sureños' soccer field
    where he pounces into their match
to break a kid's nose;
    it spews out blood
faster than I have ever seen.
    It soaks his shirt.
I can't look away.

CAST IRON

Again, the doctor removes
the ingrown toenail. Eighth grade,

Dad gardens in the backyard
when the cast iron plancha falls
from the bent nail onto my big toe.
The doctor says I need wider shoes.

Infection. The nail turned black.
Blood wept from the cracks.
Dad just watched. He said *It's time
for you to act like a man, and stop*

your crying—I tell the doctor
I want to see the procedure done,

the clippers tearing through the nail,
ripping it out from the flesh.

The doctor pierces my foot with the needle.
Even numb I still hear you.

TO SING

I secure a sheet of drywall with a screw gun.
The loud whirl cuts through the ranchera music
blasting from a small boom box.
The constant dance of hammers
& the sawing out of covered sockets,
like a song against song. The only time beatings stop
is when the day ends covered in dust.

The next day I return with my father,
my hand unable to grip. He smiles
& I force my fingers around the base
with one squeezing the trigger
to punch the sheets with black screws.
The arm's bruising muscles don't respond
as he glares under his brows. The shake
of my hand severs the gun from my grip.

SOCCER PRACTICE

It's tough to walk
on concrete and asphalt.
Dad knows cleats are made for grass.
Still, he sends us, the bench,
to chase the balls into the street
where the cars swerve and honk
to sideline us. Have you ever tried
to run on ice? He encourages us to cheer
during the games on Saturdays.
The white chalk on the grass
like barbed wire coiled around the pitch.
The color of my jersey the same hue of red
as my teammates'; the sweat is absent
on mine. On the sideline
we wear orange vests like children
in the woods during hunting season.
We run extra laps around the field
during the scrimmage at the end
of practice. A ball flies over the fence
and I run after it into the street
where a red car ejects me
with a honk and a middle finger.

DRYWALL DUST

The drywall dust settles on my skin.
I can't hide from it. It finds me
like the cold air that chills my face
through the window I just sawed open.
I desire desk work while my hammer pounds
to the beat of Vicente Fernández's "Volver Volver."
My dad, in the other room, sings.
I smash my thumb and call it a day.
Outside, the sky, clouded and dark,
holds back the rain.

THE CALL

My mother calls.   She says my father has collapsed
        holding his chest.   That I should leave
immediately   to join her
            in the waiting   room as he is rushed
                into surgery.

                Another punishment of his?

I pace the kitchen,   the phone in my hand,
        the speaker cracking   my mother's voice into the vast distance
between stars hidden by daylight.

Out the window a man   pushes a shopping cart   full of groceries
        into the alley   and a dozen roses   streaming yellow
from the child's seat   while his daughter,   maybe 4 or 5,
        straggles behind him.

        With no hurry to his steps,   his posture gives way
                to the weight of light   beaming over the Sierras.

His daughter skips   then kicks a loose rock   down the alley,
        bouncing off a garage door   with a clang. He doesn't stop

to tell her to settle down.
     He doesn't beat her with his belt
         like my dad did,
              the one embroidered with his initials,
             the one he used to brand
                   my body when I was loud
                        and didn't follow his orders.

     He hands her the dozen roses   to hold.
         The glass vase   huge in her hands,
         the petals in her face,   against her eyes.

     My mother's voice fades when they disappear.

II

AFTER ONE YEAR OF TRYING

I stumble into the kitchen,
eyes still in the haze of a dream,
to start a pot of dark Folgers coffee.
She likes it strong so I add an extra spoonful.
The coffeemaker begins to hiss.
The smell of the brew wafts through the cold
apartment. My wife emerges from the bathroom
with a look on her face that says *not this time.*
When I brush my teeth I check the wastebasket
and look at the "not pregnant" display on the test.
We watch TV, the traffic reports and the news,
together in silence, both of us with steaming mugs
in our hands. The diesel engine
of the neighbor's truck begins to roar.
Another neighbor's car door slams.
Through the window, I see their routines.
On the couch, we interlock our fingers.
Then she goes to put on her makeup
in front of the bathroom mirror
as I stand and shave next to her.
She straightens her hair while I tie my shoes.
Her perfume, fresh and strong,
a mixture of berries, a smell I've grown accustomed to
over the years, and I know it's almost over.
She stands by the door. Without looking
I know it's 6:58 a.m. I get up and go to her. We kiss,
a peck on the lips, as if somehow
with this small gesture of affection
we might both return to that dream.

WASHING DISHES

The plates that stood overnight in the dry sink
are canvases of neglect . . . bits of fried flour,
burnt butter, and pasta left to dry like stucco.
Leftovers stick like bad memories,
like the biting words, *irresponsible*,
childish, and *selfish*. My wife and I left the table
to scream each other's faults down the hall.

I turn the faucet on, and the hot water
fills the crowded sink, loosens the grime.
I remember the hard clinks of forks against dinner plates.
The water runs across the faces of dishes
clasping onto the bits of fried flour
as if breath was leaving for good.
And maybe I should leave too, grab the keys and disappear
into the bright lights of L.A. And never come back.

My father once told me, *marriage is hard work*.
I didn't believe him, but I should have taken to heart
the hard grasp he had on my hand when he shook it and told me.
I'm not going anywhere. I know that.
I'll be here in our apartment later tonight.
I'll make a chicken stir-fry for dinner. And we'll
make cold stares at each other while using only
the necessary syllables to speak a demand—
Put away the dishes. Go outside to smoke.
Take out the trash. And then we'll add *Please*
and the word will be forced like eating vegetables
because we both work hard. These hands know that.

INHERITANCE

The woman who crafted
the table, her palms cracked—
the way a riverbed turns
barren—sands her calluses
to find the life hidden
and stuck in the crevices.
When she sold the table
she ran her fingers over
the rounded corners
and said, *I left it all here.*
For ten years it stood its ground
in my parents' living room,
surviving the spills of milk
from bowls, to be given
as a gift to me when I left.
The sturdy frame remained
even after the ploys
of three boys who claimed
the wood each as their own;
I had stood on the stump and proclaimed
to be more capable than my father,
a giant literate in its grains.

Now, the coffee table leans
to the left. Its leg loosened
by a bolt that went missing
in the move. The weight belongs
to the oak and the yellowing
newspapers stacked
as high as my belly.
The awkward tower
filled with the devastation
of all our neighbors
has yet to bear the names
of the children I pray for.
My wife says I should sell it.
But I recycle the papers,
wipe the dust, replace
the bolt, and study the lines
I once said I could decipher.
I run my hands gently
over the stained surface.

PRAYER

Reading *polycystic ovary syndrome*
from lab results, the ink permanent,
my wife's eyes lose their blue
trying to understand the dyslexia
of her body; the confused twitch
of her brows shake
the language I speak
from my tongue. Did You see us burn
the copy we took home,
the blackened shreds floating like moths?

I pray—leave us alone.
Let us walk to the bus stop without the shrill
of all the kids we can't have
playing at the daycare on the corner.
The laughter.

HOLLYWOOD ENDINGS

The moths thaw out from the lamppost
to soften the yellow
like the lights before a movie starts;

the dark, held back
by the glow of the screen,
lingers like a hungry bat.

I don't know how much longer
these nights will last;
the walls have suffered enough
from the naming of faults.

We don't talk about Hollywood endings.
We stopped watching movies together.

The moths are too faithful to the light.
And when it flickers I envy
how they dance in the dark.

My wife shifts in her sleep,
and I hear her teeth grind
like a carcass dragged
slowly over gravel.

MUSEUM OF NATURAL HISTORY

Outside, the wall's
concrete cracks
spread all over

as if they were nerves
on its skin. Inside,

the library of decay,
the stuffed rabbits
and fauna stuck
behind a fluorescent amber

for style, holds its breath.
I learn that fungi will outlive us all.
They predate the structure of bones.

We are born without clothes;
for warmth we kill for skins.
And it's cold this morning.

SKIN

A place one returns to

when the sky is as dark as asphalt

with the smog that hovers over Blackstone

and rattles the foundation

of our small apartment, cramped

with the clutter of each other.

Then breath begins

to fog the window of air

between us. I am home.

NEED

Looking at you I know my body is not mine.
The shade of red on your lips
makes me think of Shelley's monster.

My left hand is a thief's. These thighs
from a woman who walked the streets
under the yellow teeth of lamps.

I thought your tongue would stitch
me into someone new. But there is an earthquake
off the coastline and a tsunami is building—

a wave heavy with fish and shit
and sand: *I love you* is not enough
to keep me together; my fingernails

keep getting bitten off during meditation.
You tell me I worry too much about my dreams
of bodies floating down the L.A. river.

I say, *I want a life baptized—*
You say, *Even me?*
I say, *you haven't been listening.*

III

DESIGNATED DRIVER

I drive my drunk aunt home
in her Hummer, and she says
things like *my daughters don't curse;*

I smoke weed with them.

She says, *I own a custom home,*
       two horses, & three stores.

I say, *I have an education.*
Though our pockets are empty.

I pass a struggling Greyhound bus
& a doe spilling its guts against asphalt;

I take comfort that we're alive as animals.

I MAKE MY FIRST DELIVERY

I find a house that used to be;
swallowed up by a fire
with forgotten furniture scattered around,
the empty rooms swell with rainwater.

This half house, half tomb,
no bigger than the one I grew up in.
Even the rust-colored trim that remains
is the same. I knock on the door
that swings open by itself.

A short man stands in the doorway.
His face, a father's, with gray hair.

I could smell that wine was his blood.
It once filled the bottles that lined the shelves
of his home. He reminds me of drywall dust.

He complains about the co-pay
and all I hear is my father's voice
burn about how his father wasn't around.
How he left him under an uncle's care.

The coals of his hands tremble
as the man reaches into his pockets for change.
His hands covered in ashes.

A pile of black and brittle lumber stacks high
on the front lawn. My father cursed his father
as he bought his own house.

It survived a fire of its own
when the garage went up in flames—
his diploma, the glass that held the degree,
warped under the intense heat.

The smoke stained the walls and ceiling.
The water from the fire trucks
soaked the furniture. Only the garage
and part of the kitchen were burned.

This house, the roof is gone.
He rebuilds as he hands me the cash.
My father rebuilt after he was abandoned.
He tried a different hand, but
how could he ever know how to love another man.

AT THE ENTRANCE OF A BACK ALLEY

After Gary Young

A teddy bear leans on a telephone pole.
Bright red balloons read "Happy Birthday."
A candle, half melted, still lit, burns black
the top of its glass. The Virgin Guadalupe
stickered with the "$1.99" price tag.
This street altar for a young boy
is all that remains of his childhood—
a bear soaked with rain and covered in grime
not much different from the one I lost years ago;
he was dark blue with white patches.
I had replaced his eye with a button
when it fell off after a wash. His color
fading over the years. This teddy's eyes are new;
they didn't see the boy facedown
in a pool of his own blood,
the wound in his chest pouring
the red and dark love from his heart.
The news says that the boy was searching
for a toy. When will I learn to let it go?
The dark bruising patches
of what once was my childhood.

MONSTER

Black men are gathered by the doorway
of the apartment I'm headed to.
Inside the delivery truck I call
the customer and leave a voice mail
reminding her that we don't deliver after dark
to Crystal Fall Apartments. They look
at me on the phone. I look at their shoes.
The way the laces are tied and their color
matter out here like the color of their shirts
and their skins. Inside this gated complex
the iron bars aren't that different from a prison's.
Inside here, shoes matter
because if I do decide to step outside this truck
and head toward that doorway I must
not step on theirs. My brother was jumped for his
Nikes by men like these, with shoes like theirs.
Brand names can be stitched on. Fakes
can easily be distinguished. My brother,
his face swollen and scratched. His mouth bleeding
from all the teeth knocked loose from the gums.
He stayed home from school for one week
and I heard him say the N-word and mean it.
I know how to mean it too. Before I leave,
I look for my brother's shoes on their feet.

MOLTING

In the wheelchair, she can't weigh more than 120 pounds.
With a Camel 99 filling the air with smoke, an oxygen tank
behind her, her hand shakes, the burning tip like a fuse.
I wonder how much we both want to meet our ends—
I return to this doorway and don't mention the cigarette
and the oxygen tank, how dangerous it can all be.
The adrenaline rush of teasing death. I hope
the explosion will get rid of these skins I live in:
the skin of man, the skin of student, the skin of husband.
Her fuse reflects my unlit fuse; no more expectations.
Again, I return to the doorway.

A WAGE-CLAIM CONFERENCE IN FRESNO

Driving from Riverside, I hit 90 miles per hour
before I downshift, gears whining
down the steep grade like an F-16 Falcon.
The car slows a little and I hear the tires
holding themselves together for all they're worth
against the asphalt. The long tail of car lights
glazes the road as I descend into the San Joaquin,
and a sense of urgency spills through the spreading night
and onto my eyes like the fumes of gasoline . . .
I pull off the 99 and onto a deserted road,
where farmland stretches for miles in either direction;
I park next to a peach orchard and close my eyes
for a few moments before I hit the road again,
and begin to imagine tomorrow's conference:
a cramped room, my previous employers
in their JCPenney business suits looking irritated
and foul, claiming they don't owe me
one red cent, though they skimmed hours
and overtime off my time cards for years.
They have a lawyer. I could afford only the full tank
of gas to get here. I'm nervous, afraid. My heart pounds
inside its cage next to a peach orchard where the croaking of frogs
serenades from the nearby canal as I fling the fallen peaches
covered in grime through the leaves, into the darkness—
I hear the slapping sounds of branches and the thud
of them crash-landing, on the fertile ground.
Every car will one day know the inside of a junkyard,
the guts of wires spilling out like these branches.
Should I turn back? How hard would it be
to forgive what was stolen?

The car's emergency lights blink as I continue to throw
the peaches harder and faster into the trees.
I will not be a coward; in the glint of moonlight
I get into the car and continue the drive,
the peaches left out to bleed and rot under the trees.

AT THE UNEMPLOYMENT OFFICE

I overhear someone say dancing is like making love.
      I think it's like riding down a long toboggan slide,

water splashing and moments of cool.
      The news says today is the end of winter.

Birds will come with their nests.
      What a distraction. There is work to be done.

I need dirt beneath these fingernails.
      I need grease stains and bits of flour

powdered onto the bottom of a shirt
      from slapping out pizzas all day.

I wear an old work hat stained with sweat,
      a memory of an oven at 525 degrees.

The weatherman explains the rise in temperature.
      There is a moment of silence before a chorus of groans

grows like a protest on the precipice of violence;
      the power likes to take hourly vacations into the Sierras

to climb the giant redwoods and bring back the breeze
      of the A/C once it has had its fill. Too many people

I don't know. We all share that same anxious look
      filled with the murderous intentions of the dark.

WASH

The caked dirt washes away
in streams falling off the car.
A milky mud drains into the gutter.
Some pools in small dents
in the pavement, pressure and time.

Drive on asphalt long enough
& it will groove to the tires.

These cloudy oases remind me of my neighbors
who wouldn't share their pool
that sounded lonely over the brick fence
most summer days in Fresno.

The neighbors' kids did not like us
and their parents didn't like the loud corridos
my dad played when he gardened.

With a pressure washer the dust comes off easy,
but I still need the brush to scrape what's left.
The tiny pools become clear as the sediment settles;
almost as clear as the neighbors' pool.

When the swamp coolers stopped humming,
my brother and I covered in sweat,
we gathered slingshots and dirt clods
& took aim from our tree house
built out of scrap lumber
and started belting the kids in the pool.

Each splash was followed by a mushroom
of dirt & blood underneath the surface.

Their shrieks jumped the fence
& an eye began to swell.

We laughed in our tree house
until my father, powdered by drywall dust,
came home from work & dragged us down
from that tree house by our ears
to the front of the neighbors' door
where we confessed through tears and snot.

We mowed their lawn over the summer
and watched them drain the pool,
the water streaming down the pavement
with streaks of mud left over
to remind me of what I've done.

The heat will evaporate the water
and leave what remains of the dirt
for these tires to kick up into the air.
Baptism isn't enough.

FENCES

You already know where the ghetto is.

There are fences around their front yards:
chain-link and around five feet high.

Some are iron bars with spikes.

And the dogs behind them growl
even when I deliver medication two houses down.

I leave the front gates open just in case

a pack of Chihuahuas flies out from the backyard,
mouths open and hungry.

There is a fence around this neighborhood,

but you already know that. You already know that
this used to be my home. You already know

not to drive south of Olive. Don't think

for a second we forgot who built this gate.

IV

—

THIRST

After Cormac McCarthy

I shoot you

for the last   gallon of water

on the shelf.   Your sacrifice

unleashes   the terror

in your eyes   and burrows

deep

into my trembling face.

The butterfly   of blood

spreads   its wings.

And the hand   of the boy

you held,   his name

will be my name.

LIZARD BLOOD

My grandfather asks me to drink lizard blood.
"It's good," he says, "gives you ganas."

I gag, but I swallow
the warm and slimy liquid down

and don't protest. The bitter taste
lingers in my mouth like the words

of my poli-sci teacher at Clovis Community
who said I should drop his class,

that I wasn't going to pass, and that I would need
near-perfect scores on all my exams.

In that office, I didn't put up a fight;
I studied while I slapped out pizzas.

"I don't feel anything," I tell him.
My face contorts in disgust while

I rinse out the taste.
My spit stained purple-red.

The headless reptile lies across a rock.
I passed that class without this blood.

No other tongue will determine
which myths I accept.

"Now you have ganas," he says. A smile across his face
as he throws the bloodless body into the bushes.

STONES

My grandfather warned me
to be watchful of scorpions
as we walked through the cemetery,
and that the dead remember everything.

He asked me to find his name
as we looked at gravestones.
I did, and then he told me about his first son,

and about the stone water tank that collapsed
and crushed his abdomen—this uncle I never knew.

The doctor had said not to give him water,
that he would fade into heaven faster that way.
He begged the doctor to save him. He begged God.

He said my grandmother held the small body
in her arms. His son repeated, *Mamma, I'm thirsty.*
Water, please? My grandmother couldn't refuse

her little boy's last wish. He brought him
water in a small cup. He showed me how he buried
his first son. I remember the sun against the gravestone,

the heat of the small lettering of our last name,
the corrosion of the first rendering it almost illegible.
He asked me to grab his hammer and pick.

He said how he stopped believing in God
as he taught me how to carve out a name.

DIET

I step onto the scale, look at the bathroom mirror
fogged with steam, and wait for my weight to flash
on the digital display in those rigid lines.

My brother reminds me that this is not my first fight.
Stretch marks curve down my torso from pits to waistline—
off-color stripes of skin tearing.

At the doctor's office I stood on the scale
and was asked to step off because I weighed too much.
"350+" wrote the nurse. The doctor writes *morbidly obese.*
The hustle of worms waits for me. I have lost before.

I tried the Medifast diet and nearly collapsed
under its 1000-calorie restriction. In the kitchen
I would measure eight ounces of chicken breast
and a cup of steamed brown rice for dinner.
I ordered pizza on the 22nd day.

Before I married I lost 20 pounds.
Then gained it back and more. This body climbs
and falls on the rails I build, but the scale is not the one
that will buckle underneath the stress.
I can't run because of a bad knee.
I show up early on the first day of class
to pick a desk I won't get stuck in.
I check the width between the chair
and the writing surface.

I see the blur of this body in the mirror,
a glimpse of my phantom
as "303" appears on the display.

This is not my first fight. The stretched skin
wrinkles without the fat, and my pants don't fit.
I grab a knife and ruler to measure
the next hole on my belt.
I drive the knife through the leather.

330-POUND MAN EXERCISES

I walk up a steep hill and smell the barbeque
from Smokey Canyon. I miss food:
a Western Bacon Cheeseburger from Carl's Jr.,
a thick-crust ExtravaganZZa pizza from Domino's,
a pack of KFC's popcorn chicken.

The charcoal smell pulls at my stomach.
I climb slowly, like the rides at Six Flags
where my wife and brother enjoy their day.
When I weighed 250 I barely fit on the Batman ride.
The man next to me, his harness wouldn't lock.

I saw the looks of disgust, the faint whispers and laughs
from the people waiting. I knew that embarrassment
from elementary school where the kids shouted *marshmallow man;*
Mister Blimp. The smell of tri-tip seduces my nose.

Drivers honk and yell out their windows, *faggot* and *fat ass.*
My brother and my wife enjoy the roller coasters,
and I follow the smell to the restaurant.
I eat at the bar, beyond the view of windows,
afraid that I may catch a glimpse of my reflection.

BOWL

My brother heaves into the toilet
as if this would stop him
from being like the men before us.
I give him water.

My father picked up his father
from the local bars filled with smoke
& the clang of billiards
& dragged him home
only to watch his body reject
like my brother does now.

I make sure he doesn't choke,
the same way I did after Pops puked
& crawled into the hallway to pass out.

I wait for my brother's gags to stop.
When he sleeps, I put him on his side.

I make sure he isn't going blue,
getting cold. This is when I clean
what didn't make it; their bodies
withering against cold tiles.

PICA

I drink beer from a tall glass with water spots.
An argument brews between the couple
at the end of the counter. I remember this tone
coming from my mother yelling at my father for spending
nights after work at his friend's auto shop, drinking.
Mother flung a glass full of beer at his head.
It missed and hit the back of the house
shattering across the red painted cement
of the back porch. I walk across the glass
sparkling under the porch light like stars
to the toolshed. I grab the push broom and sweep
the shards and beer off the porch.
I sit in the chair until the screaming stops.
The bouncer escorts this couple out
of the bar, and the light from outside
blinds me for a second like my father
when he told me *married people fight.*
And how, *I shouldn't tell others about*
what happens in our home. Darkness returns.
I don't remember if the trash bin or
my mouth swallowed those shards.

THE MEASURING TAPE OF A DRESSMAKER

In her small shop that faces the cobbled stone
she sells dresses to quinceañeras and brides.

Her dresses add color to the landscape:
a pale white dress on a dark skin bride, hair black,

her curves unyielding in the grasp of the measuring tape.
The stitches hold together the twirling fabric

that unfolds like a fist opens into a palm.
She says that in her shop no woman was ever denied beauty.

While she sleeps, I grab the tape from her shop
and measure my body.

LAST WORDS

I want to be cremated when I die. This is why I'm losing weight.
If you're too fat, they won't do it.

The body fat acts like oil and burns everything;
even the smoke dissipates into nothingness.

I don't want to lie in a box as if I'm sleeping,
lying to the people coming to see me, giving them a glimpse
    of hope
that I may still rise, and breathe, and laugh, and reminisce

about all the shit I did and all the shit I'll still say I didn't do
but I did or maybe I didn't.   Only God knows.

        .   .   .

I left that Catholic god a long time ago. Although, I still believe in
    a god,
but not this Catholic one or that Mormon one, or whatever one
    you think is right
and whose rules I have to follow, regardless of which name you
    may call Her.

        .   .   .

But my story hasn't been told. It hasn't even begun
and I'm already talking about cremation and death.

I have tons of family in Chicago. I've never met them,
but they know of me because of my grandmother
and her attempts to visit everyone before she dies.

.   .   .

What if my breath is taken away
and my wish to be cremated no longer exists
and fades like a memory?

.   .   .

Yesterday I was asked to imagine my death in the abstract.
I thought this: The firing of electrons. Brain waves collapsing,
beaches of memories, grains like breaths.

Kisses.   Handshakes.   Winks.
Bumps on a crowded sidewalk, and on buses
and in playgrounds—fouls like in soccer,
                 basketball, real soccer, football. No. Fútbol.

And story time in first grade—a green sweater
with plastic spider webbing
and the girl behind me who traces the webbing with her fingers.

Falling.

I'm bleeding like pens in pockets. I'm stains in a Laundromat,
next a five-dollar bill, forgotten, dancing with clothes,
as it slaps against the glass conga window of the dryer.

No moon. No stars. I'm in a cave in Mexico,
stalactites like fingers, outstretched, caressing, full of want.

Cookies. Milk. Oreos, and Santa Claus. The Easter Bunny.

They're all illusions.

I love you.   I think.   I once loved.

THE STONES FROM THE WATER

I.

I was spit out of Popocatépetl,
discarded like waste,
broken over and over
from mountain to boulder to rock
to this stone you threw into the water

in a tantrum. The sky accepted me
like a monarch in migration.

This water accepted me
regardless of my violent intrusion.

The lava will take me back.
Like I came into your palm.
Like I exited your grasp.

II.

You complain as if you were the first
granite boulder to be split open
by a glacier. This crack of a cry of yours,

these fragmentations from pebbles
to sand, are nothing new.

What do you know about being a father?

I was once a mountain.

III.

I disappear in the water's grasp.

Ripples string across the skin
before the placidness returns.

You think by forgetting me
you'll be able to move on?

You think to forget is to forgive?

Go ahead and pick up another stone
and throw it.

I'm still here.

IV.

You picked me up
and threw me

as if this would help you erase
those who you think did you wrong.

I was once like you—molten rock
burning everything I touched.

You are a fool.

You don't even know what forgiveness is.

V.

I accepted this beach.
I accepted your hand.
I accept this water.
I accept my erosion.
I accept the sand I will become.
I will welcome the fire.

V

AFTER HEARING OF MY FATHER'S PASSING

After César Vallejo

This afternoon it's raining in Riverside
and I remember how the mountains of Los Angeles
slowly put on their long coat of pines
as we climbed trails up the steep inclines
of the heart; breaths were hard to take.

I'm sitting here drinking coffee
and thinking of my body and its ghost;
how easy its steam rises into nothingness,
like this coffee. This afternoon the conversation is bitter.

The fake-sugar packets are all lined up
according to their color: peach orchards
in a thick winter fog. This afternoon's soft drizzle
is as insistent as memory. Its touch
I can't escape under an umbrella.

You had gone to see your father,
who still worked his land, tending to the magueys
on his hill. You stopped saying I love you
after you returned. Did you hear the slow ache
bending like a bowstring in his voice;

the loss of his first son under the crumbling rocks
of a water tank? Maybe you felt the arrow
moving through your body's landscape like a glacier.

I remember the mountains, the echo of shotgun blasts
herding quails into the sky. Father, I remember hearing you
say how much easier it would be to bury a father than a son.

This afternoon it is raining like that day I had no desire
to gut the deer hanging from the tree,
to carry the limp body over the hills,
to have its blood drip on my clothes
and dry in between my fingers.

I have no desire to lower your casket,
your body, into the ground, and watch it sway
before the hard wood of the coffin meets the soft earth.

I still remember the man who kept twenty paces ahead of me
up those mountains, who every now and then looked back
to make sure I was still there.

ARS POETICA

To hush the salt in my breath,
Neruda's palms rise from the dirt—

      the final blueprints of memory,
            pine chewed into paper.

I'm so tired of being angry—
      & the wedges of fingernails
      buried into my palms.

It's frustrating not knowing
how to build a wooden chair;

      I can write its name.

I've mutilated my body enough
trying to mimic his ascent.

      Even so, I will continue
though my hands will never be as splintered as his.

WHERE THE SIRENS GO

Mother's voice cracks when she orders us into our rooms.
A piece of wet bolillo stuck in my little brother's throat,
his lips turn the colors that choke the end of dusk.
I step on a toy fire truck and slip. The truck cracks
and the batteries spill into the hallway where Mother digs
into his mouth, her finger shaking before it disappears.
Dad, with tears on his cheeks, speaks into the phone
our address and the blue coming to lips.
The fire truck's wheels keep spinning.
I pick up the batteries as I hear the sirens
and try to put them back but the truck is broken.
I wasn't watching him like I was supposed to.
I was too into the movie we rented. Rise, damn it!
Breathe, damn it! The door opens. Firemen enter
just as my mother digs out the wet bolillo.
I keep trying to put the batteries back in
and finally use some tape my mother hands me
to patch the toy back up. I don't sleep that night.
I watch him as he dreams. His chest rises and falls.

OPEN LETTER

You, Chief Dyer, defend the badge
in front of cameras. Their lights exposing

the creases on your face
when you speak. The polygraph of skin

spells out everything I want to know—
the victim was on the phone when he jumped

over the backyard's brick fence
into the alley where small patches of grass grow,

where this supposed weapon (a cell phone) was held,
ready to fire. The news cuts away

to a man in his mid-twenties, no facial hair,
almost boyish if it weren't for the tattoos

crawling up his neck, the ink black as tar
on the streets, a dog paw under one of his eyes,

and "Bulldogs" sprawled out across his scalp.
He looks like my brother. They share those eyes

broken by the pop-pop-pop of bullets.
Who knows if my brother would still be alive

if he didn't jump to push down a girl
as a car drove by and spit up accusatory lead.

What if the angle were different and an artery burst
like a blossom? What if my brother was my cousin?

What if my cousin was just a friend? What if this friend
was another man? Or the boy who lives down the block from
    you?

What if this person was your brother
who jumped that brick fence to hear the voice of his lover

only to hear the silence inside the barrel of your guns?
Behind a podium, you defend the badge.

Your words drop from your lips like stones
into water—a small splash followed by ripples

before the calm returns—and the TV is turned off
and all of our brothers, cousins, and friends

are forgotten in the darkness of the screen.
We've become too comfortable with murder.

THE LANGUAGE OF MASA

Her fingers have danced this many times before,
like a prayer on her rosary bead.

She hums and I can't help but listen,
the calmness of the song of masa . . .

me, a pebble of sand washed away by a flood.
Her wrinkled fingers like the lines inside a tree,

each for a year she has lived, each for a child she raised,
each for a day she worked around the stove,

mastering the language of masa, taming the fire inside
and turning the tortilla over at just the right time.

I LEFT YOU A NOTE

You've stayed in the kitchen
from house to house. Does he not see
how hungry you are for your friends?
I've wondered how long you've accepted this
or whether the cold tiles of the floors
and counters have hypnotized you
over the years into believing what he does
about what your role is in this house.
I see how you look out that window.
I see how happy you are when you leave
for work, that part-time job he's allowed
you to take because we needed the money.
This isn't natural for you.
Do you know that you belong out there
beyond this view of drywall and eggshell paint.
Do you dream about using those legs and leaving?
I don't know your maiden name. Mom,
maybe you're just a dream.
I can stay, but I won't. I don't want
to see you die this way.

ADDRESSING A LETTER TO MY FATHER

After Philip Levine

First the paper will yellow
and I'll think of the dead grass
in our front lawn, the summer's
drought in its cloak of heat,
and the tart juice of tangerines.
I'll see a typewriter at an estate sale
among the porcelain statues of boys
kissing girls under umbrellas glazed with dust
and remember an old photograph of you,
the writing on the back:
"Shaver Lake camping trip 1992"
and the trout you gutted and ate
boxed in by the pines.

In an antique store there is a Corona typewriter
in a brown briefcase, and I think of your truck
with its two shades of brown, one dark, one light;
wet dirt, dry dirt. And I remember you walking
through the front door stinking of sweat,
your shoulders drooped, the creases
on your forehead like fault lines

on a map I studied in geology,
your body covered in drywall dust.
I remember the typewriter you bought me
for school, your hammer
and how you showed me to wield it.

I remember all the homes I helped build,
the drywall I nailed to lumber,
the first words I typed, "this is not a toy,"
as you dictated them to me. And I wonder
where that typewriter has gone. I keep searching
from thrift store to antique store in downtown
Fresno with its one-way streets
I wish I could disobey.

I spotted it once through a window
with Christmas lettering sprayed on in white
and I doubled back only to find
that it had disappeared. I remember
holding your hand as we exit a grocery store
into a bright day, an ice cream cone in my hand,
your thick mustache hiding a smile,
and the quarter you made appear behind my ear.
And I know that no matter how much I write
out your name, that it will fade like our voices,
that these letters are just symbols
that mean nothing to someone else
but mean the whole world to me,
so much so that even by writing your name,
Father, I will have brought you back,
to Shaver Lake where you taught me
to filet a fish, to the homes where you
showed me where to place my thumb
on a hammer, to the front of La Estrella
Meat Market where, with a simple quarter,
I will bring you back to life.

BIRTHDAY DINNER

The carpets have been replaced with white tiles.
The couches are now dark brown leather.
And all the pictures on the walls have nice frames.
In the kitchen Mother prepares mole
with the precision of a chemist,
her hands glide through the ingredients
she recites out loud like a song.
She says her mother taught her this recipe
over a woodstove and using real ground cocoa
bought fresh from the zocalo in Tilza—
generations of fingers sorting
through these same ingredients.
This wealth transferred through messy fingers.
Her hands are different, too.
Thinner. Her palms bordering exhaustion.
She says the chicken broth holds the flavor to
the secret family ingredient. I repeat this part
of the song amidst the spinning of the blender
before all the ingredients, stirred and blended separately,
come together in the center of the kitchen
to create a spicy smell that consumes the old air.
In this house a bedroom was replaced with an office.
And I know it's not much longer now.

HE HOLDS OUT HIS HANDS

He drinks another shot.
We share the crisp sighs of opening beers
as he stares at the strawberries I bought him.
How these hands, he says, used to scoop up strawberries.
How he used those hands to carry them home
to make licuados and salads. How we used to eat them
every day, with sugar or chocolate or just plain.
How that might be the only thing we ate for dinner
or lunch or breakfast. How he would steal them
and sell them door to door in the neighborhood
to buy tortillas and a gallon of milk.
How his hands were once soft and tender.
How the dirt stained them with calluses.
How he watched the sun rise every morning
and watched it work its way across the sky
like him across the fields those first years in Oxnard.
How he used to cry in the shower after work,
hot water running down his aching back
from being bent over all day. How he hid
this pain from all those around him behind those hands
as he wept in the bathroom. How he didn't know
how much longer he could go on living like this.
How he shows me his hands, his skin cracking,
his fingers thinner, dirt underneath his nails.
My hands are as big as his, these hands I've inherited.
How he holds out his hands as he begins to cry.
How he can't eat strawberries anymore.

LOST LETTER TO KEES

You on the precipice, the fog you thought was heaven,
the water sloshing around the legs of the Golden Gate,
the salt of the Pacific pressed against your lips,
the poem you were about to write with your body
and how cliché it would read in the *Times*.

On the fourth floor of the building I'm in
the beaches of Los Angeles are beyond my view.
You were tired of everyone building
a monument to greed. I know I am.

I've spent too long in a dim room
trying to type out this worthless curse . . .
That must be why you painted *After Hours*—
to separate the whirlpool from the light.
I've thought about the concrete, the ocean floor.

One day I might join you in Cuernavaca,
in a musky cantina on the city's edge—
a cold Victoria in our hands, dodging
the sunlight intruding through the open windows . . .

We'll discuss the women dancing, the jazz
from the streets of New Orleans beneath the smoke
of unfiltered Aguilas. Or Perhaps we'll eat mangos

in Acapulco with our feet in the sand, in the shade
of a cabana, the sun's brush dipping into the sea,
the constant hush of waves. You'll say, "This is all
we've ever needed," as we walk deep into the Pacific.

DUSK

After Larry Levis

My father beat a man's face
to the color of dusk; dark purples
and reds being swept over Tilzapotla.
The man, Claudio Ocampo, had just slammed
my grandfather to the ground,
a knee pressed against his spine,
over the sale of a cow that wasn't producing milk.
I heard the cracks of his ribs
as my father ran out of the house
to knock Claudio off my grandfather,
his fist unhinging this man's jaw—
the splatter of blood spit out onto the cobblestone
mixed with the dirt; a mirror of the sky.
When it was over my father and grandfather came in
and we ate our pan dulce with hot chocolate
on the second-story balcony, listening
to the crumbs falling into our laps.

On the plane back to the States,
while his hands healed from the swelling,
I asked about the fight. *I'm sorry*
you had to see that, he said.
And that's all he ever said of it.
I never understood this apology.

Sometimes, while I play football at dusk,
I stare through the cement and bricks,
the exhaust of this city in summer,
and realize I'm looking at blood again.
A small flicker drying, mixed with dirt,
and warning. It used to make me think of love,
looking at the sun dipping into the mountains.
In Fresno, that light was furious.

Now Fresno darkens as the wire
from the street lamps is stolen—my father is dying.
His hands have lifted so many cigarettes
from pocket to mouth that his breath is disappearing
like the light. When I visit I hear his coughs
wake him. They wake me.
And we sit in the cold
of the backyard looking up at the stars
and I remember my father telling a younger me
that when we died we went to heaven
and became the stars we see at night.
For years I believed we would all become stars.

Now, we don't talk about endings,
or stars, or the way his fists undid
a face. We just watch the sky
as if it could bring back breath
and love, the sparkling sugar
at the bottom of a paper bag
that once held warm pan dulce.

We both light cigarettes
and blow smoke as if we were cities
and the streets were going dark
as dusk gives way to night,
as a son shuffles from one lamp
to another trying to stay warm
and safe under their glow.

But tonight, Father, it is dark
here in Riverside, where the earth just rattled,
and the walls cracked like the bones
that night you broke dusk out of a man's face.
Yet here when I think of you, I can almost believe
that the street, as it rolls into the hills, leads to the stars.